In a Dark Place

Stories by
Carol R. Ward, Heather Horton, Heidi
Sutherlin, Jo-Anne Russell, Sarah Bella
and Jamie DeBree

In a Dark Place
ISBN 9781937477820
In a Dark Place Copyright © 2011 Brazen Snake Books
All rights reserved.

Compiled by Jamie DeBree & Heidi Sutherlin
Edited by Carol R. Ward
Cover art by Heidi Sutherlin

Table of Contents

The Box
by Carol R. Ward

In the world of the temple everything served a purpose, even her. But she had to wonder, what purpose did the Box serve? The Box sat upon a low table in the sanctuary. Looking down at it, Tessa shivered. It was small, too small really, made of some kind of black wood, carved with arcane symbols. It gave her an uneasy feeling, just looking at it, but she shook the feeling off. The Box was her only hope of salvation.

Ever since she overheard two of the attendants talking about the girl who'd managed to escape her fate, she'd thought of nothing else. All she had to do was to find some place to hide until the appointed time had passed and she'd be considered tainted, unfit for sacrifice. Safe.

Time was growing short. Tessa considered her options and there was really only one way out.

The Box. No one would think to look for her inside the Box.

The sacrifice would take place at sunset. By moonrise, Tessa would be free, a fact she kept reminding herself of as she was bathed and dressed - red tunic, representing blood, and soft green trousers, representing the earth.

"There's no need to weigh you down with the jewelery yet," one of the attendants told her. "Perhaps you would care to meditate in the garden to pass the time."

"Perhaps I shall," Tessa said with a serene smile.

She moved slowly and sedately down the paths, the attendant following at a discrete distance. The garden wasn't a true garden. A true garden had the sun shining on it from above, the wind blowing freely, the rain coming down at will. This garden was covered by a dome. The climate was strictly controlled and the trees planted in large pots to limit their height. Raised flower beds held only fully edible plants, nothing toxic. Those were reserved for a different garden, one that only a few had access to.

When she reached the fountain at the center she sank gracefully onto a nearby bench. Closing her eyes, she assumed a relaxed pose. After a few minutes the attendant began to fidget. A few minutes more and there was a whisper of sound as she moved away. Tessa's eyes opened to slits and when she was sure she was alone her eyes opened fully and she got to her feet. Quickly she followed a different path headed towards the sanctuary.

It would be a sanctuary in more ways than one, she told herself as she slipped inside. A shiver of excitement went through her. It was going to work, no one had seen her, no one had reason to suspect she had figured out the one place she would be safe. She approached the black Box—her salvation. Slowly. Reverently.

Tessa frowned. How did it open? Running her hands over the surface she felt for a latch. Ah, there. A devil's tongue, how appropriate. She gave it a tug and there was a soft click. The slightest of gaps appeared in the edge of the Box that was closest to her. Eagerly, her fingernails clawed for a hold, prying the side open. It swung forward on an almost invisible hinge.

Her head snapped up. Were those voices? Hurry, hurry, hurry. She placed one foot in the Box and recoiled. There was something not right about the touch, something . . . No time, no time, no time. Suppressing her revulsion, she forced herself into the Box.

It was a tight fit—good thing she wasn't claustrophobic. If she sat with her knees drawn up, arms pulled tight to her chest, head bent, there was just enough room. She even managed to get the side closed again, just as the voices coming towards the sanctuary grew louder. Too late. She was safe. They'd never think to look for her here. Tessa smiled into the darkness.

"Is she in there?" one of the two burly priests asked.

The attendant emerged from the shadows. "Yes, my lords," she said, bowing low.

"Good. You may go now."

She nodded again and scurried from the sanctuary.

The other priest went over to the Box and pressed the locking mechanism. He shook his head in disbelief. "It amazes me how often they fall for this."

"I'm just glad so many of them do," the first priest said. "It makes it much easier to get them to the altar. And it's so much quieter."

They looped the poles they were carrying through the rings on the four corners of the Box. Hefting the poles to their shoulders, they left the sanctuary and entered the temple.

"Makes for a much easier clean-up too," the second priest said as the settled the Box on the altar. "The god doesn't waste much."

There were noises coming from within the Box. Scrabbling sounds, like claws scratching. Muffled whimpers that might have been screams had the Box been open. And a faint, suckling noise, like something being slowly eaten.

###

About the Author

Residing in Cobourg, Ontario, Carol has always had a love of writing. She grew up reading old copies of Edgar Rice Burroughs and Robert E. Howard so it's no wonder her first love is fantasy and science fiction.

She always believed she was meant to be a writer of short stories, however her stories tended to be rather long. They also tended to have a romantic thread running through them. Finally caving in to the inevitable, she embraced her genre of began writing novels of fantasy/science fiction adventure with a dash of romance thrown into the mix. She has never regretted it.

Today she writes a variety of prose: non-fiction, flash fiction, short stories, and novels – in a variety of genres: humour, horror, contemporary, romance, science fiction, and fantasy. Having recently discovered a love of poetry forms, she explores a new form of poetry every week.

Visit Carol on her blog, Random Thoughts of the Writerly Kind.
http://randomwriterlythoughts.blogspot.com.

Within Six Walls
by Heather Horton

Melina was surrounded by darkness. With eyes shut and body trembling, she stifled her tears. The air was murky and thick and she coughed painfully between fast, shallow breaths. Her knees were drawn up to her chest and her arms were hugged around them. Her forehead rested on her knees and waves of dull pain radiated from the back of her neck to the base of her spine.

Melina was in a box.

Someone in the distance asked "What are you thinking about?"

Melina's own voice was one that she did not recognize and was shaky and coated in fear, "I'm afraid that I'm never going to get out of here."

"How long have you been in there?"

Melina tried to clear her head enough to answer the question but her mind was as dark as the space that engulfed her.

"How long have you been in there?"

"A long time," Melina responded, hugging her knees tightly.

"You know how to get out."

"I don't," Melina said, tears welling in the corners of her eyes. She was on the edge between desperation and panic as her muscles tightened from lack of movement.

Melina felt the urge to rock back and forth in attempt to comfort herself. However, the *thud* of her head hitting the wall behind her and her knees hitting the wall in front of her sounded deafening in the black space and she quickly stopped.

There was a snap. Melina's eyes opened instantly and the blackness washed away like water swirling down a drain. The walls of the box fell away. Relief rushed over Melina as if she was waking up from a nightmare. There was a moment of silence in which Melina felt like she was transitioning between two separate states of existence.

Melina found herself sitting in a familiar office. Dr. Gray sat across from her, a middle-aged psychotherapist who had soft features and curly brown hair that was pulled back from her face.

"I want you to go home and rest," the psychotherapist said with a warm smile, "it was an emotional hour."

Cool Montana air caressed Melina's skin like a whisper as she stepped from the downtown office building. As the days of autumn shortened, the falling sun in the western sky appeared to light the orange and yellow leaves on fire. The sun kissed Melina's face as she stepped onto the sidewalk. Soothing against her skin, the cool October breeze comforted her and the calm of the afternoon embraced her shoulders like a scarf.

Melina had been meeting with a psychotherapist once a week for two years to sort out the malingering effects of a troubled childhood. Her memories had been scratching against her life like tree branches scratching against the side of a house during a storm. Her painful and secretive past had kept her from experiencing life to its fullest as an adult. Her psychotherapist had been using hypnosis as a form of therapy and for the first time in years, Melina felt like she was on the right path.

She sat on the edge of her bed with a magazine in one hand and a cup of coffee in the other. Her house was quiet and comfortable as the afternoon faded towards evening. Melina took a sip of coffee from her mug and then leaned to the side to place it on a small oak chest that sat at the end of her bed. Her heart stopped as she pulled her hand slowly away from the mug handle. With lungs constricted, recognizable fear crept over her. The magazine fell to the floor between her feet.

The box.

All at once, Melina understood.

The oak chest was from her childhood and contained all the memories of a painful past that she had spent her adult life trying to forget. Within the box there were stained photographs of her family with vacant stares as well as letters sent from her father after he had abandoned the family. Her mother's journal, bound in tattered leather, recounted years of abuse suffered at the hands of Melina's father and sat at the bottom of the old oak chest.

The box, along with its contents, had slowly been suffocating Melina.

She usually draped a blanket over the box or stacked a pile of magazines on top on its lid so that she didn't have to see it and face her painful past. Now that Melina was looking at the box, it appeared to loom in her presence.

Melina stood up from the edge of her bed and walked towards the window, looking over her shoulder at the box like it was an intruder in her home. She feared the box that sat at the end of her bed because of the secrets that it contained. The contents of the box had haunted her since childhood and she wanted desperately to escape the pain.

"*You know how to get out,*" her psychotherapist had advised her.

Melina's breath caught in her throat as she focused her attention to the window. The sunset illuminated her eyes and cast a fiery orange haze over them. She looked back at the oak chest, the orange light in her eyes fading like embers in a fire. Without breaking her gaze, she reached into her nightstand drawer and when her hand emerged, it clutched a book of matches.

###

About the Author

Heather Horton currently lives in her hometown of Billings, Montana. She is a psychology student at Montana State University with aspirations to become a clinical psychologist and author. She enjoys reading, running, snowboarding, and spending time with her Chihuahua, Boo.

In a Dark Place
by Heidi Sutherlin

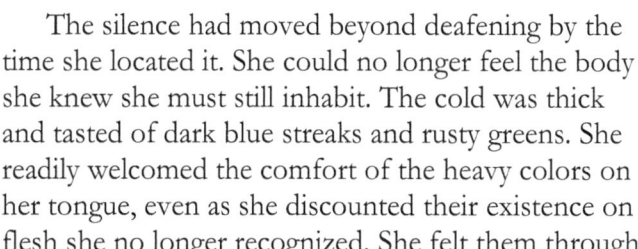

The silence had moved beyond deafening by the time she located it. She could no longer feel the body she knew she must still inhabit. The cold was thick and tasted of dark blue streaks and rusty greens. She readily welcomed the comfort of the heavy colors on her tongue, even as she discounted their existence on flesh she no longer recognized. She felt them through a mouth that no longer needed to open to function.

The weight of her solitude lifted her and she drilled her mind down, burrowing deeper into the sensation. There. She'd nearly caught it that time. Impatience was a texture she couldn't quite remember how to operate. It felt as if she'd been falling through the barriers in sensation for lifetimes. It took no effort now to hold the line taut between control and seeking. There was a nearly idle curiosity here, an inherent confidence in her absolute immersion.

For a moment only, she juggled the weight of time, wearing the notion of activity between what had been heartbeats, thoughts, testing, swirling, dissolving under the weave.

Time. An empty thump in a long line of beats, marching through, what?

There.

Focus was a bright shower of light, swirling, the center drawing blind sight. She felt a sudden clarity of curiosity as the intrusion distracted from that beat, erratic now. The empty thump, now a rattle, tasting fainter, the color, one she couldn't imagine.

Again.

Discord, flashing recognition, that was pain. Pain, inversion. Upended and swirling that which was is the other.

Unpleasant. The fibers pulling tighter, no longer balanced, no longer stretched thin, but fraying, terrible fear. Tasting colors in a scream that never reveals itself to its rational thought.

Thought. Feel. Pain.

Thump, rattle. No longer marching. Wandering now.

Wandering, aimless, beats no longer following in line. Ants, erratic.

"Crashing. We're losing her. Damn it! Where the hell is her pulse?"

Her.

Body, skin, bone.

Pain. Gasping pain, unable to clear the barrier of the nothing that was too much for her to wade

through. The marching now had long since given way
to aimless wandering, erratic beating on a singular
drum. The sound so small, she no longer strained to
feel it.

"No! You're not done. God damn it, breathe,
damn you!"

Revolving sensations spiraled into formation; one
by one falling into line with the understanding that
she had simply stepped away from. Comprehension
drifted through her in the same manner that life
seeped out. Too close. She'd been too close, nearly
touching it this time. She.

I.

I nearly touched it.

With the rediscovery of self came panic, slowly
blooming, overtaking the slow march, the steadily de-
clining beats of a heart too long disconnected from
conscious direction.

No. Please. Not yet. I'm close. I nearly felt it. So close.

Desperation gave way to horrendous pain as the
final components of thought clicked silently into
place. Senses, long thought independent of one another slammed into the forefront of her conscious-
ness.

"Stand back! Clear!"

She felt her teeth clench as blue fire lit up the
space behind her eyes. An endless amount of inactiv-
ity gave way to instantaneous reaction, full scale, as

her body arched, each receptor sending frantic reports to a suddenly overburdened nerve center.

NO! Not this way! Please...

"Pulse?! Come on! Does she have a pulse, or not?"

The march continued, beats lining up, slipping into their preordained order. Each percussion taking her closer to herself and further from the elusive clutches of insight, of discovery.

Opening her eyes, she waited, suddenly patient, while white slowly dissolved into shapes, then colors and finally to textures. She realized with perfect and instant calm that each portion of self that she'd peeled back and away had finally curled back in on her psyche. She was whole again. She welcomed the pain as she welcomed the awareness of concern in the eyes of the men and women staring frantically down at her.

As with each of the other times, she disregarded the tubes, wires and sensors snaking over her nude body. She was familiar with the dry, coppery taste on her tongue and the weakness in her throat.

"Thank, God."

The voice, this voice, was one that she knew she should feel. Turning her head to the right, looking over the edges of the black walls of the container she was suspended in, she stared up into eyes that her mind told her were familiar. She felt only cold indifference, and her reaction set off an idle alarm in her mind. She understood that she'd shifted more and more away from her original self with each immersion into the box; each time coming out further from what she was and closer to the new, to the superior.

Knowing that it would avoid complicated and uncomfortable delays, she moved the muscles of her face into a configuration that she knew he would take with comfort. She calculated his emotions, staring at him out of eyes that no longer recognized the emotion he was attempting to project.

"How long?"

"Sixteen days, four hours, thirty two minutes and forty seven seconds," came the grim answer.

She stared back calmly, the passage of time no longer important, the seeking was all that mattered now. She saw the moment that understanding passed over his face. The horror, another emotion she no longer required, animating facial muscles that were already foreign to her.

Turning her head back, she stared blankly at the dark lid, already relaxing her body, commanding muscles taut with their recent trauma to release. Closing her eyes, she gave her final command, knowing she would be obeyed.

"I'm going back in. Seal it up."

###

About the Author

Heidi Sutherlin is a writer of Romantic Suspense and Paranormal Romance, a Graphic Designer and a Cover Artist. She currently wreaks her particular brand of digital mayhem from her home in beautiful Central Oregon while riding herd on a wily four year old and a plastic addicted black lab named Frannie. To connect with Heidi, visit her web site at http://heidisutherlin.blogspot.com/

The Promised Land
by Jo-Anne Russell

Libby-May Johnson awoke to total darkness. Her legs cramped under the weight of her body. She tried to move but the walls of the cedar scented prison had her trapped in her current position. Her mind was fuzzy, and short of her own name, she couldn't remember much else.

She slammed the side of her head against hard wood as the box jerked violently up and down. She tried harder to remember. Pa had taken her to Queeny's shack for some help. She was going on a trip – one that she may not survive.

Pa had gone into the back with Queeny leaving her alone. The place smelled musty and dank of rotting wood and old blood. The roof shook as gusts of wind passed outside.

She stood and walked across the room to the wood shelves nailed to the wall. Mason jars lined them, jars filled with herbs, powders, and liquids. She reached for one to take a closer look.

"Don't you be a touching my things girl, you hear," Queeny called as she entered the room.

Queeny led Pa in and motioned for him to sit as she snatched the jar away and put it back.

"Your Pa here says you be needing my help."

"Yes, Ma'am."

"Better be doing exactly as I tell you, I don't got no time for folks that don't be minding my words. Come on girl, get to the back room and I will fix you right up."

Libby-May watched Pa drop his gaze as she passed him. She followed Queeny into the room and sat on the edge of the makeshift bed, while Queeny rummaged through an old trunk. She turned with a bottle of brown powder in her hands.

"What's that?"

"This here powder is what's gonna get you through the trip. It be just like going to sleep.."

She handed the bottle to Libby-May.

"What do I do with it?"

"When you get to the last station before the big ride, you mix in some water and drink it. Your body will slow right down to nothing, and you be sleeping the whole trip away. Mind you now, don't be drinking the whole bit, leave some in the bottom or else you be sleeping for good."

Libby-May put the bottle in her pocket and followed Queeny back to her father.

He stood and took her by the arm. "Thank you," he said, as he led her out.

They walked in silence until they came to the path leading to the station. She stopped and turned to him.

"Pa, why can't you come? "

"It's too dangerous, leaving Joe behind. I sent word I was coming, and I ain't about to not keep my word. Now you mind what Queeny told you, and follow the path. When you get there, Lewis will take you to the promised land. I'll be seeing you soon enough."

She hugged him and wiped a stray tear from her eye. "I love you Pa," she said. She kept her focus on the path walking through the woods as the sun set. Five hours of pushing through tree branches and bugs flying in her face, passed by the time she made it to Lewis' house – the last station. His wood wagon sat out front ready for the cargo. It would take her on the last legs of her journey where she would finally be free from the white man and his slavery.

Someone peeked from behind the brown curtain of the house and closed it again.

"What's your name girl?"

"Libby-May Johnson. My Pa told me to ask for Lewis."

"You Bob Johnson's girl?'

"Yes sir."

He took a look around. "You see anyone following you?"

"No sir, and I was watching."

"Okay then, come on in. We leave in an hour."

She followed him into the house and sat at the table with another woman and a young boy. Lewis gave her a bowl of stew and a glass of water.

"It's going to take about ten hours to get there, and you won't be getting out until then. If you hear anyone you can't make any sound at all, you hear?" His face wore a serious expression.

She nodded, and after asking where she could wash up, left the table and headed to the bedroom taking her glass with her. She removed the bottle from her dress pocket, and began carefully pouring the water into the bottle, when the room curtain swung open.

"You need any help?"

Libby-May twisted, pulling the bottle behind her. Some of the liquid spilled over her fingers.

"No Ma'am, I'm fine."

"Here's a towel, call if you need me."

When the woman was gone, she finished filling the bottle and put it to her lips. The aroma of sweaty feet and rotten potatoes invaded her nose. She plugged her nose and drank until the bottle was empty. She put it back in her pocket and joined the others at the front of the house.

Lewis pulled a blanket back in the wagon, and offered Libby-May a hand.

She climbed in and watched Lewis lifted the seat off the pew.

"It 's cramped, but it is the only way. You ready?"

"Yes." She climbed in and folded herself down. over her bent legs as Lewis banged the seat back down tight.

A few minutes later Queeny's mixture made her feel really sick, but she went to sleep anyway.

Now, as When she woke she knew something was wrong. She was ravished, ready to tear the pew apart to escape.

She placed her hand on the underside of the seat and pushed it up letting in the morning daylight. Her skin was grey and her nails bluish black. She threw off the seat and sprang.

They tumbled from the wagon to the ground. She growled and tore at his flesh. Suddenly she realized what she had done. Lewis's arm was in her hand, his flesh in her mouth. She was an abomination, and this wasn't the promised land, but she was free.

###

About the Author

Jo-Anne Russell is a horror writer living in Lindsay, Ontario Canada.

Her taste for the macabre has provided her imagination with a feast that fuels her writing and creativity. If you like horror, the bizarre, or you just don't like to sleep at night, give her books and short stories a try.

Her debut novel The Nightmare Project is the first in the shocking trilogy called Dangerous Minds, and is now available. For more information, please visit her web site at: http://www.jo-annerussell.ca

We Play
by Sarah Bella

I wince as the silk scarf digs into my ankles and simultaneously thank my lucky stars that Master used something gentler than the hemp rope he used last time we played.

The blindfold over my eyes blocks all light from seeping in. I've got no way of knowing where he left me this time or which box I'm in.

The ball gag in my mouth prevents me from breathing easily and makes my jaw ache. The acrid taste of new rubber makes my mouth water and I struggle to swallow.

Sensory deprivation is good for me, he says.

I need to learn to trust him fully, he says.

Good things come to those who wait, he says.

All these things he says, and more, lead to an outer sense of calm. But inside, I'm freaking out. My muscles are rebelling against the facade. It's been hours - I'm sure of it - and I can only hold back the shakes for so much longer.

I try to focus on what I do know, instead of what I don't know.

The box is small, this time, not even enough space for me to stretch out head to toe. I turn to the side and discover the box is narrower that direction.

Like a coffin.

The realization does nothing for my mental state so I suck a breath in through my nose and move on.

The floor and walls are hard, not padded. They feel rough, so they probably aren't glass, which means I'm probably not on display. Well, the box is, but my physical self isn't.

I can't feel or touch or smell anything inside the box with me.

The box is warm and I wonder if I'm in a heated room or if it's well sealed and I'm slowly heating the little box myself.

I shift back to my original position, careful to stay on my side. I know how easy it is to choke on your spit when you're wearing a ball gag.

A strand of my hair gets tucked beneath my chin and halts my movement. I fumble blindly trying to disentangle the hair where it's stuck to my sweat slicked flesh.

I know he's not far. He'd never leave me alone, not for a minute. But even as I strain my ears I hear nothing from outside the box and nothing inside the box but the thundering of my heart and my labored breathing.

I try to count my breaths as a way to slow my speeding heart and to measure time, but the focus on my breathing only reminds me how completely still and silent it is.

I am as alone as I have ever been in my life. I know the purpose of the scene is to teach me self control, a mental exercise. Restraint has never been my strong suit.

Knowing the purpose behind my seclusion doesn't help stave off the impending terror. The doubts creep in and I start picturing myself dying in the box. All the horrible ways I could die.

I could die of thirst, contorting in horrible cramps and spasms as the moisture is sucked out of my muscles.

I could suffocate when my certainly limited air runs out.

I could give myself a coronary imagining all the ways I could die.

I could choke on my own spit, for fuck's sake.

And now I know I'm going to die here, alone, in the box.

The paranoia eats at my forced calm. The tremors creep into my limbs and I can feel my fingers start shaking first. I squeeze my eyes shut harder behind the blindfold and tears seep out the corners of my eyes. The thick fabric soaks them up before they can escape down my cheeks.

I kick my feet against the box, awkwardly for the binding at my ankles. The dull pain in my heels reminds me that I'm not dead yet and my thoughts return to my list of ways to die. A final burst of frustration propels me forward and I slam my forehead against the top of the box.

Stars explode behind my eyes and a strangled cry escapes the ball gag.

Suddenly the unnatural stillness is broken. Nothing overt, no symbols crashing or sirens blaring, but the oppressive nothingness is gone.

I breathe as deeply as the panic attack allows, sucking in greedy lungfuls that burn my nose with their harshness.

"What a pretty sight." The voice washes over me and suddenly, I can breathe. The shakes subside and I roll onto my back, reaching blindly for him. His hand wraps around my bound wrists and I'm pulled upright before I can choke.

"Come on, pet, out of the box." Strong arms envelope me and lift me free of the box. I blindly loop my arms around his neck and relax into His firm chest.

My breathing slows to something resembling regular and I sigh in relief.

This is how we play.

###

About the Author

Sarah is a small town Minnesota girl who calls pop by its proper name – pop. She wrote her first novel when she was fourteen; it may or may not have been up to industry standards. She now writes both novels and short stories in the romance, mystery/suspense, paranormal and erotica genres.

She loves traveling anywhere south of the equator and finds that a nice dark microbrew can help get the creative juices flowing. When she's not writing or traveling, you can find Sarah with her nose buried in a book. Sarah lives in the small town she grew up in with her husband, three children, her cat and her dog. Visit Sarah's blog at www.shelikesitverbal.com.

Dark Therapy
by Jamie DeBree

Drip. Drip. Drip.

The woman shifted, hard metal cradling her none too gently as it leached cold through her thin clothing. She tried to stretch, first an arm, then a leg, but her limbs were bound to the chair. She blinked, straining to see through the darkness, but the black was so thick that her efforts were fruitless.

"Hello?" she called out, trying to remember how she'd gotten there. A memory flirted with her conscious mind, though the blurry images refused to focus.

Drip. Drip. Drip.

She tried to relax, breathing in and out slowly through her nose as she'd learned in yoga class. Closing her eyes, she took stock of her body, starting at her neck, and moving downward, focusing her mind on each part in turn. Unhurt, she tested her bonds, sliding her wrists back and forth underneath them and deciding the fabric was silk. What kind of captor used silken ties?

Drip. Drip. Drip.

Breathe in, breathe out. The air was surprisingly fresh in her nostrils, and carried the very faint scent of sweet oranges and cinnamon. Her stomach rumbled, hinting that she should find the source. Her ankles moved restlessly, trying to break free.

Drip. Drip. Drip.

Her bare toes stretched downward to explore within a limited reach. She was surprised to feel soft fiber against the ball of her foot. A shiver cavorted under her skin at the contrast. What was this place?

Drip. Drip. Drip.

A cool draft licked over her torso as something creaked in front of her. A door? "Hello?" she tried again, her eyes opening to peer into the nothingness. "Is someone there? Where am I? Who are you?"

Drip. Drip. Drip.

The silence roared in her ears as she waited, breathing forgotten, her pulse pounding against her neck. Someone was there – she could feel it. An imposing presence that smelled of - she sniffed the air - warmth. Musky and very male, she could feel him standing a little ways off. Watching. A brief flash of potential recognition teased her brain again, but it was gone as quickly as it had come.

Drip. Drip. Drip.

"What do you hear?" a low, gentle voice asked. He was closer than she'd thought, and instinctively she turned her head to the left, toward the sound.

"Water," she said, her muscles tense. Waiting.

"What do you smell?"

The voice was in front of her now, a disembodied anchor she desperately wanted to connect with, if only because she felt so isolated and helpless.

"Sweet orange. Spices. Warm musk."

Drip. Drip. Drip.

"Are your eyes open or closed?" he asked, somewhere behind her now.

She frowned, only then realizing her eyes were still shut. "Closed."

"Good. Do you remember why you're here?" Again, the voice had moved, now closer to her right side.

"No."

"Do you remember your name?"

Drip. Drip. Drip.

She twitched, his breath hot on the back of her neck. "Constance," she breathed, relieved to be confident of that one thing. "Constance Newell."

"That's right." Thick fingers trailed lightly over her shoulder and down her arm as he moved in front of her. His hands rested on her wrists, not a tight grip, but she felt the inherent strength in his palms. "There's something I need you to do for me, Constance. Something that only you can do. If you're successful, I'll bring you a great deal of pleasure. Would you like that?"

His thumbs caressed each of her arms in slow, hypnotic circles as she nodded, unable to fathom anything less than obedience.

His voice murmured low in her ear, his presence all-consuming for several moments.

Then he was gone.

Drip. Drip. Drip.

Opening her eyes, Constance blinked and held a hand up to block out the sun shining through the window of her office. Shaking her head to clear away the cobwebs, she yawned, reaching for her coffee cup. This was the third time she'd drifted off in as many days. If she could just sleep at night…but the fear was too great.

Turning to her computer screen, she put her fingers on the keyboard and then froze. She had to go downstairs. Right *now*.

She pulled on a white coat from the rack by her door and hastily affixed her credentials. Heels clicking against the gleaming floor, she went to the elevator and selected sub-basement two. It stopped on level five, and Dirk Ellison stepped in beside her. Her pulse sped up at his male scent, though he'd always intimidated her. She considered getting out, waiting for the next car. But she couldn't delay.

"Hello, Constance," he said as he pressed the button for sub-basement one, his deep, calm voice triggering an inexplicable moisture between her legs.

She nodded his direction, thankful he didn't pursue conversation.

Finally stepping out of the elevator, she made her way through a dim, concrete hall, her steps echoing eerily. Two rights and a left, then down a short flight of metal stairs that required her to stay on her toes, lest a heel slip through the mesh. At the bottom, she stopped, a familiar voice whispering through her head.

I'll bring you a great deal of pleasure.

If only, she thought as she approached the black room-sized box, her steps less confident the closer she got. Reaching into her pocket she found a key, though she couldn't remember where she got it.

Would you like that?

Yes. She unlocked the door, stepping back as it swung open. Darkness was the only thing that greeted her. She'd been afraid of the dark since the attack, but she needed to enter the box. To go to him. He would protect her. The urge was almost strong enough to overcome her fear.

Almost.

She turned away, frustrated tears in her eyes. Strong hands held her as a needle pierced her arm.

"One more time, love." Dirk's gentle eyes were the last thing she saw before she drifted to sleep.

Drip. Drip. Drip.

###

About the Author

A full-time webmistress by day, Jamie DeBree writes steamy, action-packed romantic suspense late into the night. Her goal is to create the perfect blend of sensual attraction, emotional tension and fast-paced adventure, similar to the television crime dramas she's hopelessly addicted to.

Born in Billings Montana, she resides there with her husband and two over-sized lap dogs. She reads in a wide variety of genres including romance, erotica, action/adventure, thriller, horror and literary fiction.

For information on upcoming books, visit JamieDeBree.com.

Rattles Flash Fiction

In a Dark Place (Oct. 2011)

At the Water's Edge (Nov. 2011)

The Old Sofa (Dec. 2011)

www.ingramcontent.com/pod-product-compliance
Lightning Source LLC
Chambersburg PA
CBHW050915120626
46552CB00004B/1591